EPIC FICTION ANTHOLOGY
VOLUME 1

Epic Fiction Anthology
Volume 1

KYRIA NAKITA

Contents

Broken Trust

India, 36, a marketing executive with curves that broke necks and a smile that shattered hearts, had it all—or so it seemed. Her career was thriving, her social media accounts were filled with perfectly curated snapshots of glamorous events and exotic vacations, and she lived in a loft that looked like it belonged in a high-end design magazine. On top of all that, she had been dating a charming and successful architect. Malcolm was everything she thought she wanted: intelligent, attentive, and driven. He treated her well, made her laugh, and seemed genuinely invested in their future together. India had everything she had prayed for... until, one night, she reached into his coat pocket and found something unexpected.

"Girl, you won't believe what happened last night!" India yelled through her cell phone, slamming her coffee cup on the counter.

"Ooooo, tell me everything!" Keisha said eagerly, settling in for what promised to be an earful.

"He's married, Keisha!!! Married!!!"

"That bastard!!! How did you find out???"

India released a deep sigh. "I was looking for my keys in his coat pocket and found a wedding band!" she sniffled.

"Oh my god, girl... So what did he say?"

"He said it was complicated, that they were separated but not divorced yet. Like that makes it any better!"

"Right! If that was the case, he should have said that!" Keisha added. "And what "separated" man still carries his wedding ring??? Get the F outta here!"

"Exactly what I said!!! We have been together for almost a year!!! A whole damn year! And you're still carrying your wedding ring??? Yeah, okay" she rolled her eyes.

"For real! Kick him to the curb. You don't need that kind of drama in your life, India. You deserve so much better than some liar who can't even be honest about his status."

India burst into tears at the thought of her relationship coming to an end.

"It's ok, boo." Keisha's tone softened. She could feel her friend's pain through the phone, and it broke her heart to know she was hurting. "Come over after work, I'll cook dinner for you."

Days rolled by, but India's feelings remained a tangled mess. She ended things with Malcolm the same night she discovered the truth, blocked his number, and erased any trace of him from her life. But as the days turned into weeks, India's sense of closure never came. Instead, she was left with a whirlwind of emotions she couldn't sort through. She fluctuated between anger at him for deceiving her and frustration with herself for not seeing the signs sooner. There were nights when she cried herself to sleep, the uncertainty of his lies pressing down on her chest like a stone. Other times, she felt a simmering rage, a need to lash out at something, anything, just to feel in control again.

She tried throwing herself into her work, taking on extra projects, and staying late at the office. She thought if she kept herself busy enough, she wouldn't have time to think about him. But even in the midst of meetings and deadlines, her mind would wander back to Malcolm—his smile, his touch, the way he made her laugh. She hated that he still occupied so much space in her thoughts, that even after everything, he had the power to affect her like this.

Her friends encouraged her to move on, suggesting nights out and introducing her to new people. India tried to put on a brave face, to laugh and pretend she was fine. But every time she saw a happy couple or heard someone mention love, it felt like a punch to the gut. She couldn't understand why she couldn't just let it go, why the thought of Malcolm still haunted her. She had been betrayed, plain and simple. So why did she feel like she was the one who had lost something? Then, one evening, her phone buzzed. It was a message from an unknown number.

I need to talk to you, Meet me at our place. 9 p.m. Please India.

She rolled her eyes at the text, knowing it was from Malcolm. Her mind raced as she stared at the message for a few moments. Her heart began to beat faster as a mix of anger and anxiety flooded her veins. *What could he possibly have to say that he hadn't already lied about? Why couldn't he just let her move on?* A part of her wanted to ignore the message altogether, to delete it and move on with her day. But another part of her, the part still tangled up in the mess of unresolved feelings, was curious.

India tossed her phone on the couch and paced the living room, her thoughts swirling like a storm. She thought about all the things she should say to him, all the anger and pain she had bottled up since the night she found his ring. She thought about how satisfying it would be to finally have it out, to lay everything on the table and walk away with her head held high. But then she remembered the look in his eyes whenever he talked about their future, the way he held her and made her feel like the most important person in the world. That was the Malcolm she had fallen for, not the man who had hidden an entire marriage from her. Her phone buzzed again, another message from the unknown number:

I know I don't deserve your forgiveness, but please, just hear me out.

Running her hands through her hair, India groaned in frustration. She felt torn. She knew she shouldn't go, knowing nothing good would come from meeting with him. But deep down, she also knew she wouldn't be able to rest until she heard what he had to say. Against her better judgment, she decided to go.

India glanced at herself in the mirror. Her red eyes from sleepless nights, old T-shirt and leggings stared back at her. She frowned. If she was going to face Malcolm, she didn't want to look like she'd been drowning in her own misery. No, if she was going to meet him, she would do it on her terms—looking confident and untouchable. She marched to her closet and put on a sleek, black wrap dress that hugged her curves in all the right places and made her feel powerful. Pulling on her favorite heels, she felt her confidence returning, layering over the hurt and confusion like armor.

Next, she sat at her vanity and applied her makeup with precision, highlighting her almond-shaped eyes and adding a bold, red lipstick that always made her feel fierce. She ran a brush through her curls, fluffing them out until they framed her face perfectly. By the time she finished, she barely recognized the woman staring back at her. She looked strong, composed, and, most importantly, in control. India took a step back, giving herself one final look. She didn't just want to be cute; she wanted to be unforgettable. She wanted Malcolm to realize exactly what he had lost and know that he could never have it back. With a satisfied nod, she grabbed her purse and headed for the door.

When she arrived, Malcolm was already seated, looking like the ghost of guilt incarnate. His shoulders were slumped, his hands fidgeting nervously on the table, and his eyes were fixed on the untouched Henny and Coke in front of him. He looked up as she approached, and for a moment, India could see raw remorse etched into his face. His normally confident posture was gone, replaced by a man who seemed to be unraveling.

India took a deep breath, steeling herself as she made her way to the table. She refused to let his appearance soften her resolve. She had spent too many sleepless nights grappling with the betrayal, and she wasn't about to let a pitiful expression erase the hurt he had caused. As she reached the table, she paused, giving him a long, hard look before finally sitting down across from him. Malcolm opened his mouth to speak, but no words came out. He looked as if he was struggling to find the right words, his throat bobbing as he swallowed hard.

"You..." he rubbed his head. "You look good."

"I know." India folded her arms across her chest, raising an eyebrow, making it clear she wasn't going to make this easy for him.

"Thank you for coming." He reached into his jacket pocket, pulled out a thick envelope, and placed it on the table between them. "I got a divorce," he smiled, tapping the envelope. "Now we are free to be together."

India's thoughts raced as she stared at the envelope. Part of her wanted to grab it, to open it and see for herself that it was true. But another part of her, the part that had been so deeply hurt by his lie, felt nothing but emptiness. She looked back up at Malcolm, shaking her head slowly.

"Malcolm," she sighed, biting her lip. "It's too late."

"India, please," he pleaded, reaching across the table. "I know I messed up, but I love you. I've always loved you. I made a mistake, a terrible mistake, but I've done everything I can to make it right. Doesn't that count for something?"

"I don't doubt that you love me, Malcolm. But love isn't enough when it's built on lies. Trust is everything."

"Baby, please!" Tears welled up in his eyes, and he dropped his head, hands trembling as he clutched the divorce papers.

India fought back tears as she watched him, but she knew her decision was the right one. She stood up, slinging her purse over her shoulder.

"I'm sorry, Malcolm. I just... can't be with a man I can't trust. And what if we were to ever get married? I would always have this in the back of my mind..."

"India, don't do this," he begged.

"I have to go. I really hope you find what you're looking for, but it's not going to be with me."

As she walked away, she felt a mix of sadness and relief. It hurt to say goodbye, but she knew she was choosing herself, choosing her own peace over the uncertainty of a future with a man she could never fully trust again.

Driving home, her phone buzzed; it was her doctor's office reminding her of an appointment she'd forgotten. Her emotions were still raw from seeing Malcolm again and she wanted to cancel. But she knew she needed to keep the appointment—she had been putting off her annual tests for far too long. Maybe it would be a good distraction, a way to shift her focus away from the chaos of her love life and onto something she could control.

The next day at the doctor's office, India sat in the waiting room, flipping through an old magazine. She wasn't really reading it, just turning pages to keep her hands busy. Her mind kept drifting back to the conversation with Malcolm, replaying every word, every expression on his face. She had meant what she said about not being able to trust him, but that didn't make it hurt any less. When her name was called, she was led to a small, sterile exam room where the nurse took her vitals and asked a series of routine questions. India answered automatically, her thoughts elsewhere.

"Sit tight, the doctor will be in shortly," the nurse said, patting her leg before leaving the room.

As she waited for the doctor, she pulled out her phone and began scrolling through social media, hoping for a distraction. But instead, her screen filled with notifications—dozens of messages from an unknown number, all coming through one after the other.

Her finger hovered over the block button. She knew she needed to cut him out completely, but a part of her still hesitated, the wound too fresh to fully close off. Suddenly, the door opened, and her doctor stepped in, holding a file in his hands. As soon as she saw the look on his face, her heart began to race.

"What is it, doctor?"

"India," he began, his voice calm but grave, "we've completed your tests, and..." he paused and looked her directly in the eyes. "You're pregnant."

The room seemed to tilt slightly, the words echoing in her ears as if they were spoken from a great distance. "Pregnant?" she repeated, her voice barely more than a whisper. Her mind raced, trying to process the information. This was the last thing she had expected, the last thing she had prepared for. "But...but you said it wasn't possible, that I'd never be able to get pregnant."

"I remember, India," he took a deep breath, nodding sympathetically. "Your previous tests showed that it would be extremely difficult for you to conceive naturally but sometimes, the body surprises us. It's rare, but it happens."

India sat back in her chair, her mind spinning. For years, she had come to terms with the idea that she would never have children. It was a loss she had grieved privately, a reality she had accepted, even if it wasn't what she had wanted. Her heart clenched as her thoughts turned to Malcolm. How could this be happening now, just when she had decided to walk away from him forever?

"I don't... I don't know what to do," she whispered. The tears she had been holding back began to spill down her cheeks, and she buried her face in her hands, overwhelmed by the weight of it all.

"It's okay to feel overwhelmed, India." He rested a comforting hand on her shoulder. "This is a lot to take in, and you don't have to make any decisions right now. Take some time, think it over, and we'll be here to support you with whatever you choose to do next."

India nodded, trying to steady her breathing. Everything had changed in an instant, and she didn't know what to do next.

That night, Keisha leaned forward, eyes wide in shock as India recounted the meeting with Malcolm, the doctor's appointment, and the fact that she'd been told she couldn't have children.

"Girl, this is a whole new level of complicated," Keisha sighed, pouring another glass of wine. "I guess you won't be needing this!" she laughed, grabbing India's wine glass.

India managed a weak laugh, but her eyes were distant, focused on some point beyond the room. "Tell me about it," she muttered, rubbing her temples. "I mean what are the odds of this happening now and with Malcolm of all people!"

"So, what are you going to do?"

'Well," India stared at her reflection in the mirror on the wall, the weight of her choices pressing on her. "I've always wanted a child," she said softly. "Maybe this is life's twisted way of giving me what I want." She sighed, feeling the truth of her words settle in her chest. "Malcolm doesn't have to be a part of it. I can do this on my own."

"If anyone can do it, it's you." Keisha hugged her. "You're one of the strongest people I know and I will be here to help you every step of the way."

"Thanks, hun."

Weeks later, India sat in her apartment, nails tapping the phone screen. She had been thinking about this moment for days, debating whether or not to tell Malcolm about the baby. She knew it would be a huge decision—one that would change everything. Finally, she typed out a message:

We need to talk. It's important.

She stared at the screen, her heart pounding as she waited for his reply. It came within seconds:

Of course. When and where?

India hesitated, thumb hovering over the keyboard. She thought about the future, about the kind of life she wanted for her child. She imagined the complications, the potential for more lies and betrayal. Did she really want to invite that kind of uncertainty into her life again... into her child's life?

As all the different outcomes churned in her mind, she suddenly made a decision. Her thumb moved swiftly, deleting the conversation, and re-blocked his number. She couldn't risk putting her child through that kind of pain. Her hands shook slightly as she sat her phone down, but a sense of calm washed over her. She had made her choice. There would be challenges ahead, and she knew she would forever wonder if she made the right decision. But for now, she was doing what she felt was best for herself and her baby.

THE END

The Reverend's Daughter

In the sultry heat of a small southern town, the steeple of the First Baptist Church pierced the sky, a beacon of unwavering faith. With her vibrant polka dot headscarf and sketchbook in hand, Naomi Monroe, sat beneath the shade of an old oak tree in the town square, her eyes capturing her world in strokes of charcoal. The tree's sprawling branches offered a brief respite from the relentless sun, its leaves rustling softly in the afternoon breeze.

Her fingers danced across the page, bringing life to the town's familiar scenes. Her eyes shifted from the church to the cobblestone path winding through the square, where children played a lively game of tag, their laughter echoing through the streets. Across from her, Miss Hattie, the town's unofficial historian, rocked back and forth on her porch, her knitting needles clicking rhythmically as she glanced up occasionally, watching Naomi with a knowing smile. The air was thick with the scent of magnolia blossoms and the faint aroma of fried chicken wafting from Mrs. Johnson's diner down the street. She paused, lifting her head to take in the scene, her eyes falling on a young couple sitting on a nearby bench, heads close together, lost in whispered conversation.

"They look so happy," she whispered. "I hope I find a love like that one day..." she sighed.

"Naomi!" her father, Reverend Elijah Monroe, beckoned, his voice a mix of affection and reproach. "You should be helping with the church fundraiser, not daydreaming out here!"

She looked up from her sketchbook, the charcoal pencil pausing in her hand. She saw her father standing at the edge of the square, his broad shoulders framed against the backdrop of the church steeple. Reverend Monroe was a commanding presence, his sermons filled with fire and brimstone that reverberated through the hearts of his congregation. But Naomi's world was painted with colors her father's eyes couldn't see, hues of imagination that stretched far beyond the church's reach. Where he saw the path of righteousness, a straight and narrow road paved with scripture and duty, she saw a canvas waiting to be filled with the wonders of the world. She found beauty in the mundane—the chipped paint on a picket fence, the wildflowers pushing through cracks in the sidewalk, the way sunlight filtered through the leaves of the trees. These details, so easily overlooked by others, were the threads that wove her reality together.

"Dad, I'm not daydreaming!" she rolled her eyes. "It's my art, my future! Why can't you see that?"

"Don't make me come out there and get you, little girl!" His voice thundered across the square as he stormed back inside, the church doors slamming shut behind him.

Naomi sighed, lowering her sketchbook. She knew her father's outbursts were just his way of showing concern but knowing that didn't make it any easier.

"Your art... it's like a window to a different world," a strange voice said behind her.

Startled, she jumped and spun around to see the source of the voice. Stand there was a tall, sun-kissed, chocolate man. His eyes were dark and deep, holding a mysterious intensity that drew her in. As he stepped forward, she couldn't help but notice his well-built physique. She felt a flutter in her chest as the sun illuminated the contours of his muscles through his fitted t-shirt.

"Oh, sorry, I didn't mean to startle you," he said with a small, apologetic smile. His voice was deep and smooth like butter. The words drip from his supple lips like honey on a warm day.

At a loss for words, Naomi bit her lip, momentarily caught up in the sight of God's glory. Her heart raced for reasons she couldn't quite understand.

"Are you ok?"

"Oh, yes... yes!" she answered a little breathless. 'I just... wasn't expecting anyone."

He chuckled, his eyes not leaving hers. "I couldn't help but notice your drawings. You've got a real gift."

"Thank you," Naomi blushed, glancing down at her work, suddenly feeling self-conscious.

"You really captured the essence of this place." He leaned in to get a closer look.

"Thanks... Sometimes, I feel like the only one who sees it differently."

"That's a rare gift," he said, moving closer. "You're really making it come alive."

Naomi smiled sweetly and looked out at the town, wishing she was elsewhere.

"Name's Marcus," he offered his hand.

"Oh, uh, Na...Naomi!" she said shyly, shaking his hand gently.

The moment their hands touched, she felt a jolt—something familiar, yet distant. She stared at him for a second longer, trying to place him. His name didn't ring any bells, but there was a familiarity in how he carried himself and how he looked at her. She couldn't shake the feeling that she'd met him before, even though she was certain they hadn't.

"Elijah, I'm worried about Naomi," her mother mumbled watching them from the window. "She's so different from everyone here, she doesn't fit in like the others."

Deep in thought, preparing for his sermon, Reverend Monroe glanced over at his wife. "She's a Monroe, she'll come around to our ways," he responded firmly. "Give her time."

"So, what brings you here, Marcus?" she asked, studying his face for some kind of clue. "I haven't seen you around here before."

"Just visiting some family," he said with a shrug, his eyes flicking briefly to the church behind her. "But I didn't expect to find such beauty in a place like this."

Naomi laughed softly, "We're not all just fire and brimstone, you know," she teased.

"I'm starting to see that," He grinned, his smile lighting up his face in a way that made her stomach flip. "Maybe you can show me around sometime. Let me see this place through your eyes."

Her heart skipped a beat. "Maybe," she looked nervously at the church. "I'd like that."

And so, over the next few months, Naomi and Marcus's relationship blossomed. What began as a casual friendship built on a shared appreciation for art and individuality soon deepened into something more intimate. They met in the secluded corners of the town square, where the shadows of the old oak trees offered them privacy from the prying eyes of the small-town yackety yaks. Their conversations stretched long into the afternoons, filled with everything from deep biblical discussions to light-hearted jokes. Sometimes they would sit in comfortable silence, simply enjoying each other's presence. With each passing day, Naomi felt herself drawn to Marcus in a way she had never felt before. He made her feel seen and understood like she belonged in a world outside the boundaries of her father's church. She found herself eagerly awaiting their meetings, her heart racing every time she saw him walking across the square. He was unlike anyone she had ever met.

Marcus opened up about his past, offering glimpses into a life far removed from the narrow streets and rigid traditions of Naomi's small town. He spoke of the places he had been—cities bustling with life, quiet towns nestled between mountains, and stretches of open road where the horizon seemed endless. Each story was filled with the freedom and adventure Naomi had only dreamed of. She listened with wide eyes, hanging on his every word, imagining she was far away from the small town, where her father's voice no longer dictated her life.

"I guess I've always been searching for somewhere to call home," Marcus confessed one afternoon. "My mom raised me on her own, and we moved around a lot. It was just the two of us, but she made sure I never felt like I was missing anything. She was tough but kind, always putting me first. I guess that's where I get my independence from."

Naomi was drawn in by the tenderness in his voice when he spoke of his mother. She could see it in his eyes—the struggles they must have faced together, the bond they had formed through years of hardship. It reminded her of her relationship with her mother, though it was so different in many ways.

"Where is she now?" Naomi asked softly, laying her head on his shoulder.

Marcus hesitated for a moment, looking off into the distance. "She... uh, she passed a few years ago," he said quietly, rubbing his head. "Cancer. I wasn't there when she died—something I'll regret for the rest of my life."

Naomi's heart clenched at his words, a deep sympathy washing over her. She reached out, placing a hand on his, offering silent comfort. "I'm sorry," she whispered, feeling the depth of his loss.

"Thanks," he nodded. After a long pause, he continued, his voice steadier. "I guess after that, I didn't really have a reason to stay in one place. I've been moving ever since, looking for something that feels right, you know?"

"Yeah, I get that," she said as she absentmindedly traced the edges of her sketchbook, her mind drifting as she glanced over at Marcus. "So... how old are you?"

"Uh..." he raised his eyebrows, a bit caught off guard. "How old do you think I am?"

Naomi smiled, rolling her eyes at his deflection. "I don't know. That's why I'm asking."

"I'm... twenty-three."

"Twenty-three, huh?" she raised an eyebrow. "I would've guessed a little older."

"Older? So, you're into older guys, huh?" he teased, leaning back on the bench.

"No, I didn't say that!" she laughed, shaking her head.

"What about you? How old are you, Naomi?"

Naomi's heart quickened, the moment she had been dreading finally arriving. Her fingers tightened around her sketchbook as she bit her lip, trying to appear casual.

"Eighteen," she said, the lie slipping out as smoothly as his had.

"Eighteen," he repeated, nodding slightly. "You look a little younger than that," he teased.

Naomi laughed nervously, brushing a stray curl behind her ear. "Well, I'm not a little girl anymore," she said, hoping her words sounded more confident than she felt.

"Well, we're not too far apart right?"

Naomi nodded quickly, though the truth gnawed at her.

"Age is just a number, anyway," Marcus said, his voice dropping to a whisper as he leaned a little closer. "What matters is how we connect, right?"

"Right," she whispered.

As Naomi's relationship with Marcus deepened, whispers began to swirl through the quiet streets of the small southern town. It started innocently enough—passing glances, curious eyes watching the two as they sat together. But soon, those glances turned into knowing looks and knowing looks into murmured conversations behind closed doors. The town, steeped in tradition and gossip, was always quick to judge anything that strayed from the norm, and Naomi's growing relationship with Marcus was no exception just because she was the Reverend's daughter. The rumors spread like wildfire, fed by the town's insatiable appetite for scandal. Women at Mrs. Johnson's diner would huddle together at the counter, their voices hushed but urgent as they pointed and speculated on the nature of their relationship.

"Have you seen her with that man?" they would say, shaking their heads disapprovingly. "She's far too young to be carrying on like that, and with someone like him?" The church ladies, always the gatekeepers of moral propriety, were even more vocal in their condemnation. "She's the preacher's daughter, for heaven's sake. Why is the Reverend letting her carry on like that?"

Naomi was no stranger to the eyes that followed her wherever she went. The judgment and the whispers, were all part of the suffocating atmosphere of the town, a place where everyone knew each other's business, and sins were never forgiven, only buried. But this time, it was different. This time, the weight of the gossip pressed down on her like never before, each rumor another thread in the web, wrapping tighter around her.

And yet, she didn't care.

The town's disapproval only fueled her defiance. She craved how Marcus made her feel—free, unburdened by the expectations of her father, her family, and the church. Their secret encounters became her escape, the only place where she felt she could breathe without the suffocating gaze of the town on her shoulders. Marcus was her taste of freedom, but that freedom came at a price. Soon, her father began to hear the rumors. Initially, he said nothing, but she could feel the tension building in their home. His sermons grew more fiery, his eyes searching hers for signs of rebellion. Her mother grew quieter, watching her daughter closely, with a mix of concern and disappointment, unsure how to reach her.

Naomi started to lie more as the meetings with Marcus became riskier. She was starting to enjoy the thrill of secrecy laced with the fear of being caught. They meet in more hidden places by the edge of town, where the fields stretched out toward the open road, or in the shadowed corners of the town square late at night when the streets were deserted. But no matter how careful they were, the town's eyes were everywhere.

"We can't keep doing this forever," Marcus said one evening as they sat by the riverbank under the fading light. "People are starting to talk, Naomi. Your father—he'll find out eventually."

"I don't care what they say. Let them talk."

For a moment, neither of them spoke. The air between them was thick with unspoken truths, with the knowledge that their relationship, as it was, couldn't last forever. But in that moment, neither of them was willing to face it.

"That girl is just too wild," Naomi overheard a congregant whispering one Sunday after church.

"You know they are talking about you, right?" Kelli, her long-time friend nudge her shoulder.

"Whatever," she spat, clenching her fists. "They don't under-stand anything beyond these walls!"

"Just be careful, Naomi. You don't know anything about him," she reminded her

"You're just jealous, KeKe. Marcus understands me!" Naomi clapped back, brushing her off.

"Jealous??? Wow, Naomi. I guess I'll talk to you later. Seek God." Without waiting for a response, she turned on her heel and walked away.

Naomi rolled her eyes, pushing the interaction aside as she turned to kiss her mother goodbye.

"Where are you off to, dear?"

"Oh, I was going to grab a coffee and head home." Naomi lied, forcing an innocent smile.

Her mother's gaze lingered, clearly unconvinced. "Ok, I expect you to be on time for dinner." Her eyes narrowed as she stared daggers into her daughter.

"Yes, ma'am."

As soon as she was out of sight, Naomi rushed through the winding backstreets to their secret meeting place. The words of the church member, Kelli's warning, and her fiery response echoed in her mind, stirring up a whirlwind of doubt that battled inside her. When she finally arrived at the meeting place, Naomi stopped to catch her breath, her hands shaking as she adjusted her clothes and ran her fingers through her hair. Pulling a tube of red lipstick from her bag, she applied it with trembling hands, hoping the color would give her the confidence she needed. She took a deep breath and turned the corner, ready to slip into the comfort of his embrace.

"NAOMI!" her father roared, standing there with his arms folded. "What do you think you're doing young lady?"

Looking like a deer in headlights, Naomi froze, unsure of what to do or what to say.

"I know what you have been up to! I will not have my daughter involved in such scandalous behavior! You will end things with this boy!"

"You can't control who I love, Daddy! Marcus is–"

"LOVE??? LOVE!!!" He cut her off with a bitter laugh. "You think you love this boy? And let me guess, you think he loves you, huh?"

Tears welled up in her eyes, his words hitting her harder than she expected. She honestly didn't know if Marcus loved her but she was sure about how she felt about him.

"You... you don't understand, Daddy!" she choked out.

"You're blinded by this... infatuation," he began to pace back and forth. "You're sixteen! Stop trying to grow up so fast! You will have plenty of time for boys when you're older!"

"But Daddy?" she pleaded.

"You think this boy—this MAN—cares about you in the way you think he does?" he began pacing back and forth. "You are a child, Naomi. You don't know what love is."

"I do, Daddy!"

"END IT, OR I WILL! And wipe that whorish lipstick off your face! Out here embarrassing me in front of the whole town!" he growled, storming off, leaving her wallowing in a pool of tears.

Moments later, Marcus appeared. "Naomi, what happened?" he asked, rushing to her side.

"Daddy said we can't be together," she sobbed, wiping her eyes. She could barely catch her breath, her emotions swirling in a chaotic mix of fear and defiance.

"Why not?" He frowned, throwing his hands in the air. "He doesn't even know me!"

"Do...Do you love me, Marcus?" Her eyes searched his face, her heart pounding in her chest as she waited for his answer. It was a question she had been too scared to ask before, but now, with everything on the line, she needed to hear him say it.

Marcus paused for a moment, the weight of her unexpected question sinking in. His eyes flicked over her tear-streaked face, her smudged lipstick, and her raw vulnerability.

"Of course I love you," he finally said, gently wiping the remnants of smudged red lipstick from her chin. "We can't let your father dictate our lives. We are meant to be together, this can't be the end!" He grabbed her hands. "We can leave this place and start somewhere new, just you and me!"

Naomi's eyes widened, her pulse quickening at the idea. Could it really be that simple? The thought of running away with Marcus, leaving behind the stifling judgment of the town and the suffocating expectations of her family, sent a rush of excitement through her. For a moment, all her fears dissipated, replaced by the possibility of a new life—one where she could finally be free.

"You really mean that?" she whispered, eyes full of longing and uncertainty.

"Yes, Naomi, I mean it. There's nothing for us here but judgment and restrictions. You...we deserve a chance at happiness, away from all this," Marcus affirmed. "We can build a life together, on our terms."

Naomi blinked back fresh tears, her mind racing. The idea of leaving everything she'd ever known behind was terrifying, but the alternative—staying and losing Marcus, being forced to live under her father's oppressive control—was unbearable. For the first time, she saw a future that was hers to claim.

"Okay," she sniffled. "Let's do it. I can't bear the thought of being apart from you, or living under everyone else's expectations anymore."

Marcus nodded, kissing her hands. "Tonight, then. I'll arrange everything. We'll leave this town and never look back."

"Wait. I can't tonight. I promised my mom I would be at the fellowship dinner on Friday night but we can leave right after!" she assured him.

"Alright. Friday night, then," he said, rubbing her back and pulling her closer to him. "You shouldn't be alone tonight, though. Come back to my place."

Naomi hesitated for a moment before nodding, she had never spent the night with a boy before. But she knew she needed the comfort and understanding that only Marcus could provide. They stood up, clasping their hands together, a united front against the challenges they were about to face.

Once they arrived at Marcus' modest apartment, it was clear that luxury wasn't a part of the evening. In the small, cramped kitchen, he prepared dinner for her. The scent of hot water and instant noodles filled the air, the steam rising from the stove as he stirred two Styrofoam cups of chicken-flavored noodles. Beside the noodles sat two slices of plain white bread on mismatched plates. The meal was simple and far from the romantic dinners Naomi had once imagined. She was accustomed to her mother's home-cooked meals.

"I know it's not much, but I wanted to make sure you ate something." He smiled slightly, handing her the cup of noodles.

"Oh... thank you," she chuckled taking the cup from him. "I've never had this before so it's... perfect," she said grateful, although her stomach twisted with uncertainty.

Sensing her unease, he gently pulled her close, his muscular arms wrapping around her waist. "Don't worry, I'm here. You're safe with me," he whispered.

As they sat at the small kitchen table, the conversation flowed naturally with Marcus sharing stories and listening attentively to Naomi's hopes and dreams. They laughed, shared their fears, and talked about plans for the future. They talked for hours, weaving together the fragile fabric of a life they both wished for.

After dinner, they moved to the thrifted, worn loveseat in the living room, the dim light from the small kitchen casting soft shadows across the room. The space between them felt charged, a heaviness hanging in the air that neither of them could articulate. She had never been this close to a boy before, not like this, and the unfamiliarity made her heart race in both thrilling and unsettling ways. Marcus leaned in first, brushing a gentle kiss against her lips. His touch was soft and unhurried, and Naomi's body instinctively leaned into him. But as their kiss deepened, her mind raced with conflicting thoughts. His hands traced the curve of her back, pulling her in closer. The nerves in her stomach tightened as a quiet voice in the back of her head told her this was moving too fast, that she wasn't sure if she was ready.

His hands began to explore her body more boldly, caressing her breasts and grabbing her butt. When he put his hands down her pants, Naomi's breath hitched, and she pulled back slightly, breaking their kiss. Her naive eyes searched his for reassurance.

"Marcus... I don't know..." she whispered, covering her mouth.

"It's okay," he said, gently brushing a strand of hair away from her face. "We don't have to do anything you're not ready for."

Naomi bit her lip, torn between her desire for Marcus and the nervousness gnawing at her. She cared about him—wanted to be close to him—but this felt like such a big step, one she wasn't sure she was ready to take.

"We can take it slow," he reassured her, softly stroking her arm.

Marcus leaned in again, kissing her more softly this time. She kissed him back, trying to push away the doubts, wanting to trust their connection. Gradually, their kisses grew deeper again, the warmth between them building. Naomi's nerves began to give way to the flood of sensations—his hands, his breath, the way he looked at her like she was the only person in the world.

"It's okay, I've got you," he whispered, lowering her on the couch.

Swallowing her apprehension, Naomi nodded. She let herself be swept up in the moment, letting go of her reluctance for a little while, trying to convince herself that she was ready. Before long, they were undressed and tangled in each other's arms, their bodies swaying together as they made love for the first time.

"Wow! I never imagined my first time would be like that!" Naomi panted, skin still tingling from the experience.

"Wait... your first time, first time?" Marcus sat up, face twisting in disbelief.

"Yes, I was a virgin," she said shyly.

"Oh, wow! I didn't know virgins still existed!" he laughed.

"Whatever!" she playfully hit him with a pillow.

"Uh, so..." he searched for the right words.

"What? What is it?" she looked at him confused.

"Does... that... mean you're not on birth control?" he winced. "Because... I finished inside of you."

"What? I told you to pull out!"

"I know, I know, but I couldn't. It was too good!" he kissed her shoulder.

"Marcus! What if I get pregnant? I can't take care of a child right now!" she anxiously buried her head in a pillow.

"Don't worry, I will take care of you and our baby," he rubbed her stomach.

"Don't do that!" she snapped, quickly pushing his hand away, "It makes it sound like you did it on purpose." She glared at him from the side of her eye.

"Relax," he sighed, pulling her against his chest. "Did you believe me when I said I love you?"

"Yes." she huffed.

"Then trust me when I say, I got you, okay?" He kissed her repeatedly on the neck causing her to giggle.

"Okay! Okay!" she screamed, laughing uncontrollably.

Friday came quickly, and they prepared to go to the fellowship dinner. Naomi hadn't been home in days and she wasn't sure how her parents would react. Despite knowing her father frowned upon their relationship, she decided to bring Marcus as her plus one. It was a bold move, a statement of defiance and commitment to the path she had chosen.

The day before she had snuck in her house when she was sure her parents were doing community outreach. She chose a simple yet elegant number from her mother's closet that reflected both her sense of style and the woman she was becoming. The dress hugged her frame in all the right places, its spaghetti straps and deep burgundy color were a contrast to the usual muted tones and modest attire expected at church gatherings. Marcus dressed in a simple suit, she snagged from her father's closet, that complemented her dress perfectly.

"Are you sure about this?" Marcus asked, adjusting his clothes, nerves fluttering in his stomach. "I don't have to go."

"Yes. We have to do this." Naomi nodded. "I can't hide from them forever."

"Alright then."

The walk to the church felt like an eternity. She clutched Marcus's hand tightly, her palms damp with nervous energy. As they neared the building, Naomi's heart fluttered. The parking lot was full of familiar cars from everyone in town who had known her all her life.

"This is it." He squeezed her hand. "Ready?"

"Ready," she whispered through heavy breaths.

The gravel crunched under their feet as they nervously inched toward the entrance. Entering the fellowship hall, Naomi held her head high, her grip tightening on Marcus' arm. The soft murmur of conversation ceased almost instantly as heads turned, one after another, as they moved further into the room. The church ladies, who had always watched Naomi from afar with disapproving glances, now openly gossiped in hushed tones. Attendees exchanged knowing looks, their eyes darting between Naomi and Marcus, trying to piece together the story they had only heard fragments of.

Reverend Monroe's eyes found them the moment they walked through the door. Naomi's heart skipped a beat at the sight of her father's harsh gaze burning into her. But she forced herself to keep walking, her body rigid with tension. This was no longer about avoiding his wrath, it was about standing up to it.

"Naomi, what are you doing?" her father hissed at Marcus, as they approached.

"Hi Mom... Dad," Naomi replied, nervously avoiding her father's question.

"Sir," Marcus spoke up. "I–"

Reverend Monroe held his hand up, signaling for silence. "You don't speak here!" he spat. Marcus just stood there frozen, unsure of what to do next. If looks could kill, it was his last day.

"IS THAT MY SUIT???" he roared, looking Marcus up and down.

"Daddy! I can explain!" Naomi threw her hands up, standing between her father and her first love. Whispers rippled through the room as their confrontation began to draw a crowd. Sensing the situation spiraling, Naomi's mother gently placed a hand on her husband's arm.

"Enjoy the evening, dear. We will discuss this later." She patted his hand as he muttered profanities under his breath, his anger far from quelled.

Naomi exhaled shakily as they walked away, relieved that her mother stepped in. The air was thick with judgment, every snicker and glance added to her anxiety. Suddenly, Marcus stopped walking.

"What is she doing here???" he gasped, turning away.

"What? Who?" Naomi said, looking around.

"MARCUS!!!" An older woman yelled, waving vigorously from across the room. "MARCUS!!!" His body stiffened as he tried to hide his face.

"Who is that, Marcus?" Naomi inquired, pulling at his arm. As she got closer, she noticed the striking resemblance between her and him. The same deep-set eyes, the same sharp cheekbones, and the same rich, chocolate skin.

"Mom, what are you doing here?" he asked, looking at her puzzled.

"Mom??" Naomi blurted out. "You told me your mother died!"

"Died? Excuse me, little girl." She pulled Marcus to the side. "I have been trying to contact you for weeks, Marcus! You haven't been answering my calls, so I came as soon as I could," his mother replied, her eyes darting between him and Naomi.

"I... I lost my phone traveling here and I haven't gotten another one yet." Marcus sighed, shifting uncomfortably.

"Well, I thought you were dead!" she put her hands on her hips.

"I'm fine, Mom," he groaned, pulling her into a hug, attempting to calm her down. "Mom, look, this... this is Naomi Monroe, my... girlfriend."

Naomi smiled at hearing him call her his girlfriend for the first time. But before she could respond, her father grabbed her arm.

"Naomi! I am not done talking to you about this boy!" he barked. "You are sixteen years old! You don't–...

"Monroe?" Marcus' mother interrupted, her face draining of color.

Hearing the familiar voice, he slowly turned around. "P-PATTY???" he stammered, grabbing his chest as he immediately recognized Marcus' mother. He hadn't seen her in years, not since their brief, secret love affair over thirty years ago. The memory of those days flooded back to him like a tsunami, a chapter of his life he thought was long closed.

"Sixteen?" Marcus mouthed to Naomi, her face flushing with shame as she felt the full weight of her lie.

"This... this is your daughter, Monroe?" Marcus' mother's voice trembled, looking from Naomi to her father.

Pale and shaken, all he could do was nod.

She inhaled shakily, the truth too heavy to hold back any longer. "Marcus," there's something I have been meaning to tell you."

"What is it, Mom?"

Patty swallowed hard, eyes filling with tears as she grabbed her son's hands.

"Reverend Monroe... is your father."

THE END

Played

K endra sat alone at her favorite lounge, Velvet, her fingers tracing the rim of an untouched drink. The warm, dim lighting bathed the room in a soft glow, and the smooth notes of jazz flowed around her like a soothing balm. She smiled at the couples sitting across from her. The clinking of glasses and the hum of quiet conversations were enough to melt the stress away. She closed her eyes and thought about the last time she and Leon were there. They sat at a cozy corner booth talking and laughing for hours. Her phone buzzed on the table, snapping her back to the present moment.

Working late again. Sorry, babe.

Again! Kendra fumed, feeling a storm of annoyance as she stared at the message. It was the third time this week he had bailed on their plans. She slammed her phone down and took a deep breath, trying to push the frustration away. Slumping down, she leaned against the plush velvet chair, closing her eyes to let the music drown out the growing disappointment gnawing at her. Her phone buzzed again. Kendra rolled her eyes and glanced at the screen.

You need to see this!

A text from her friend, Tasha, flashed across the top. Curious, she swiped the message open and her heart sank instantly. She held her breath as a video played of Leon, at a bar with his hands resting comfortably on a woman's butt. The woman smiled and leaned into him. Without hesitation, he bent down and kissed her passionately. Kendra felt the sting of tears at the corners of her eyes, threatening to spill out. Her grip tightened on her phone as she looked around. The comforting music now sounded like distant noise, echoing in a hollow void. Exhaling slowly, she sat the phone on the table, willing herself to relax.

"Fancy meeting you here," a familiar voice said.

Startled, she turned and saw Darius, Leon's brother, looking down at her with a smirk.

"Mind if I join?" he asked, already pulling out a chair and sitting down without waiting for her response.

"Uh, sure," she replied, quickly locking her phone and slipping it into her purse.

"What's wrong?" He leaned back, eyes narrowing as he studied her. "You seem off."

She rolled her eyes at his question, he was the last person she wanted to confide in. Feeling a sudden urge to numb herself, she signaled to the bartender for three more shots. Darius watched, amused as she tossed back her freshly poured whiskey.

"Woah! Going hard tonight, huh?" he chuckled.

"What do you want, Darius?" she snapped, slamming her shot glass on the table.

Darius shrugged. "To forget, maybe... Just like you."

"Assumptions can be dangerous."

"Fair enough," he said, leaning forward slightly. "But I know, it's not like you to hang out here alone. Where's Leon?"

At the mention of Leon, Kendra's heart tightened. She had always been leery of Darius, never liking him much. He had a reputation for being a player, always cheating on his girlfriends without a second thought. She could never understand how he and Leon were brothers—they were so different. Or at least, she had thought so until tonight.

"Not here," she answered dryly.

Darius nodded, seemingly content to drop the subject. He drummed his fingers on the table, glancing awkwardly around the club, and waved to the bartender for another round. As the night wore on, the tension between them grew thicker, fueled by each sip they took. The atmosphere in the club had transformed; the once hypnotic dance of the colored lights now seemed ominous, casting shadows that flickered and swayed, making the room feel like it was alive and watching. Kendra bounced freely to the beat of the music. She could feel the alcohol dulling her senses, making everything inside her feel calm and carefree. She kept her eyes trained on her drink, refusing to meet Darius's gaze, even though she could feel his eyes on her, studying her, trying to figure out what she was thinking. After tossing back another shot, Darius spoke.

"I know about Leon."

Kendra froze, her eyes locking onto his. She had always prided herself on being strong, on keeping her emotions in check, but now, under his unflinching stare, she felt like a child caught in a lie.

"W...what do you mean?" Her eyes narrowed, grip tightening around her glass.

"Don't play dumb, Kendra." Darius leaned in closer, his words tinged with a bitterness that surprised her. "You think you're the only one he's stepped out on? You think you're special?"

The sting of his words hit her like a slap in the face. She had suspected Leon might have been unfaithful before, but hearing it confirmed by Darius—of all people—felt like he had just ripped away the curtain she'd been hiding naked behind. Throwing back another shot to dull the sharp edges of her pain, she searched for the right words. She wanted to curse him out and send him on his way but she knew that would only escalate negatively.

"Why... are... you.... telling me this?" she managed to say through clenched teeth.

"Let's just say, karma has a way of coming around. I say we give it a little push," he suggested, sliding his hand onto her inner thigh, his fingers warm against her skin.

"Some brother you are!" she spat, shoving his hand away.

Darius leaned back slightly, holding his hands up in a show of surrender. "Look, KeKe, I kn–"

"Don't call me KeKe."

"My bad, K..e..n..d..r..a... I'm just saying, you deserve a little get back."

Kendra stared at him, puzzled but intrigued. The alcohol was starting to take a stronger hold on her, and everything seemed to slow down, her thoughts muddled by the intoxicating haze.

"Go on."

Darius's lips curled into a half-smile. "Sleep with me. Let him find out. Level the playing field."

Feeling a rush of conflicting emotions, her breath hitched as the words sank in. The idea was outrageous and reckless, but she felt a sick sense of thrill at the thought of revenge. As the alcohol surged through her, it pushed away her inhibitions and clouded her better judgment. She felt bold and invincible. She was tired of playing by the rules, tired of being the one who always got hurt. Here was her chance to hurt Leon in the same way and show him that she wasn't someone who could be played with.

"Okaaay," she slurred. "Let's do it."

"Alright," he smiled mischievously, leaning closer, his breath warm against her ear. "Let's make sure he never forgets this night."

They retreated to a motel, a dingy place perfect for dirty secrets and whispered regrets. The door creaked as they stepped inside, revealing a room that looked like it had seen better days, maybe decades ago. The neon sign outside buzzed faintly, casting an eerie glow through the thin curtains that did little to block out the outside world. Kendra glanced around the room, her eyes lingering on the battered dresser with its chipped paint and the small, grimy bathroom visible through a half-open door. A flickering bedside lamp lit the room, casting long shadows on the peeling wallpaper, marked with stains from water damage. The atmosphere was heavy with the scent of cheap air freshener trying to mask years of indiscretions, mingling with the faint smell of cigarette smoke that clung to the curtains.

Kendra stood by the bed as Darius moved behind her, gently placing his hands on her shoulders. She took a deep breath and closed her eyes, anger still bubbling beneath the surface. Shivers raced down her spine as Darius kissed her neck, the rough texture of his stubble grazing her skin. His lips trailed slowly down to her collarbone as he turned her around, his eyes searching hers.

"We don't have to do this. I can just take you home," he whispered.

"No, I want to..."

Darius nodded, his expression unreadable as he leaned in and kissed her. The kiss was slow, tentative at first, as if he was testing the waters, gauging her reaction. He could taste the whiskey on her tongue as their kiss deepened. A small part of her screamed for her to stop, to walk away before she did something she would regret. But a much larger part, the part fueled by alcohol, hurt, and the need to prove something, took over, drowning everything else out. She reached up, wrapping her arms around Darius's neck, pulling him closer as they stumbled toward the bed. The mattress creaked under their combined weight, the springs groaning beneath them, protesting each movement as Darius pressed down on her. As the night wore on, Kendra let herself get lost in his touch, the alcohol buzzing in her veins, amplifying her emotions, pushing her forward with a reckless sense of purpose.

As they lay disheveled in the bed afterward, the room's dim light barely illuminated their intertwined forms. Kendra stared up at the stained ceiling, her mind still buzzing from the alcohol and the rush of what they had just done. She smiled, feeling a vindictive satisfaction, knowing she had crossed a line from which there was no return. The silence between them was thick, punctuated only by the muffled hum of a distant TV and the occasional creak of the motel settling around them.

Suddenly, Darius's phone buzzed on the nightstand. He reached over quickly, his lips curling into a sinister grin as he read the screen and sent a text. Without saying a word, he jumped up and slid back into his jeans, buttoning up his shirt with a quickness that made Kendra's stomach lurch.

"Where are you going?" she asked, wrapping the sheet around herself.

"To celebrate," he replied nonchalantly, not even looking at her as he pulled on his shoes.

"Celebrate what?" her eyebrows furrowed in confusion.

"My plan worked."

'What are you talking about, Darius!" she demanded, a knot of dread tightening in her stomach.

He just chuckled to himself but didn't answer. Confused, Kendra lunged forward, grabbing his phone before he could stop her. As she swiped the screen, her blood ran cold, color draining from her face. It was a text from Leon: *Is it done?* Followed by a video of her and Darius in the bed, the camera angle clearly showing her face.

At that moment, everything became painfully clear. She had been played—set up from the very beginning. The anger and hurt she had felt toward Leon now twisted into a new form, sharper and more self-inflicted pain. She had been a pawn in their game, and she hadn't even seen it coming.

"You... you set me up?" she gasped, voice trembling.

"You really thought you could get back at Leon through me?" he scoffed, snatching his phone from her shaking hand. "Yeah, we planned this. You're not a victim, so stop looking like you didn't enjoy it."

"So what was the point!" she yelled, sitting up on her knees. "Why go through all this? What did you get out of it?"

Darius paused by the door. "Leon needed assurance that you were just as untrustworthy as he is," he replied, his tone cold and dismissive. "I even gave you another opportunity to walk away. But what did you say, "I want to." Now, he can move on without feeling guilty about what he did."

"So this was all just some sick test?" Kendra asked, clenching her fists, her nails digging into her palms as she refrained from attacking him. She wanted to scream, to lash out, but she knew it wouldn't change anything.

"Yeah, pretty much," he shrugged, his casual demeanor making her blood boil even more. "Leon didn't believe that you were as innocent as you seemed. He thought if he could just give you a little push, you'd show your true self. And... he was right! AND! You know I have been trying to tap that since you got with Leon!" he added as he opened the door. "Oh, and Tasha was in on it too. She actually bet $100 that you would never sleep with me. Guess your friend doesn't know you that well after all."

Feeling a rage like never before, she lunged at him as he ran out the door. She felt so played, but the game wasn't over...

THE END

Sanctuary of Secrets

Reverend Lance Brown stood at the pulpit, his voice echoing throughout the St. John's Community Church with the kind of authority that made every listener lean in. The Word rolled off his tongue, scriptures polished and persuasive, each sermon meticulously crafted to reach the depths of his congregation's souls. He spoke of faith, redemption, and the power of forgiveness, painting vivid pictures of a life grounded in devotion to God. Reverend Brown was charismatic and righteous, a magnetic spiritual guide who knew how to inspire and captivate, offering the kind of solace people needed each Sunday.

Sitting in the front pew was his wife, Angela, the perfect image of a devout First Lady. Her beauty was undeniable, almost angelic, her hair pinned back elegantly into a low chignon at the nape of her neck. She was quiet, supportive, and never left her husband's side. To the congregation, her presence in the church was as much a symbol of reverence as the cross that hung behind Lance. A soft, practiced smile always graced her face and her eyes never left her husband when he preached. Her style was simple, yet refined, carefully chosen to project an image of modesty and submission. However, the slight tremor in her hands as she tucked a stray curl behind her, revealed more than she intended.

"Can I get an Amen?" Reverend Brown bellowed, eyes scanning the room, waiting for the wave of responses that always followed.

"AMEN!" the congregation responded in unison.

Angela let her lips form the word, "Amen," but the sound barely escaped her throat. Her eyes dropped, then flickered nervously back to Lance. The last thing she wanted was to draw attention to herself and make him angry... not again. Her trembling fingers smoothed the fabric of her dress in an attempt to stay calm as the memory of the last time she upset him haunted her. The way his eyes turned cold the moment they were alone and the disrespectful words he had thrown at her when he thought no one could hear. His smile in public was a mask, a facade she knew too well, and she had learned the hard way what happened when she didn't play her part.

In the church, surrounded by people who admired him, Angela couldn't afford even the smallest slip. To them, Reverend Brown was a man of God, a leader to be respected and followed. But in the quiet of their home, away from the adoring gazes of the congregation, his righteousness unraveled. There was another side to him, one that only she bore witness to—a side that terrified her more than she could admit. So, she sat there, Sunday after Sunday, forcing "hallelujahs" and "amens", moving her lips just enough so it appeared as though she had spoken aloud. Because even here, in the safety of the church, where people believed they were under God's protection, there was evil inside the man in the pulpit. Something she dared not provoke.

A few months ago, Angela was alone in their home, a rare quiet moment in the life of a pastor's wife. The house was eerily still, a silence that felt almost foreign after the constant bustle of church functions, meetings, and endless calls for her husband's time. She had spent the morning going through the usual motions—tidying up, preparing for dinner, folding laundry—now she finally had a moment to sit and read a few chapters of her favorite book.

Lance had left his phone on the kitchen counter, buzzing intermittently with new messages. It wasn't like him to forget it, but lately, he seemed distracted more than usual. There had been more late nights, hushed phone calls, and excuses that didn't sit right with her, though she tried to push the suspicions aside. After all, she was the pastor's wife; doubting her husband, especially a man of God, wasn't something she allowed herself to entertain. Not openly, anyway.

But that day, something was different. His phone continued to buzz, and the nagging feeling that something was off gnawed at her relentlessly, like a splinter she couldn't ignore. Normally, she respected his privacy, giving him the space he always demanded. But not today. Today, that small, persistent voice in the back of her mind grew louder, drowning out her willful ignorance.

"Holy Spirit, guide me," she whispered a small prayer as she walked to the kitchen.

Her hands trembled as she reached for his phone, pulse quickening as if her body already knew what her heart was ready to face. She unlocked it with a passcode she had seen him enter one evening as they sat together on the couch watching TV. Angela hadn't intended to notice but as he shifted, adjusting his position, his screen lit up, catching her attention. His thumb moved quickly over the screen, unlocking it in plain view. Trusting him completely, she'd never desired to know his password. Yet, now that she had seen it, it felt like a door had been left ajar, a temptation lingering just out of reach. Each time she thought about using it, she silenced the urge, convincing herself that trust was the foundation they both stood on. Peeking into his private world would betray that trust, but now, with doubt swirling around her, she could no longer ignore the need to know. As the screen illuminated, she immediately went to the incoming notifications. They were from someone named Deacon T.

"Deacon T?" she whispered, frowning in confusion, not recognizing the name.

Clicking on the text thread, Angela gasped as she saw message after message of flirtatious texts, winking faces, heart eyes, dripping lips, and eggplant emojis. As she scrolled further, her breath hitched as she reached explicit pictures of Tasha, one of the new members of the church. Tasha was talented, energetic, and well-liked. She had a way of drawing attention—especially Lance's. Angela had noticed it a few times before but had always brushed it off as her imagination, an insecurity she had no right to entertain.

Her heart hammered so hard she thought it might burst through her chest. Her mouth went dry as she continued to flick through the messages, each word felt like a sharp knife slicing through her. Lance's responses were equally damning—compliments on her beauty, suggestions to meet privately, words Angela had never imagined him speaking to another woman, let alone someone from their church. She stumbled backward as a wave of nausea hit her. *Is this really my life? My marriage? How long has he been doing this?* She thought gripping the counter for support, knees buckling as she gasped for breath in her silent, empty kitchen. All she could do was stare at the phone, mouth open, vision blurring with unshed tears. The man she thought she knew and the life they had built together... was a lie. And now, standing in the echo of that revelation, she had no idea what to do next.

Suddenly, the side door creaked open and Lance walked in. He paused, glancing at his wife's tear-filled eyes and down at his phone in her hand, still aglow with the damning evidence. His expression instantly shifted.

"Tasha, really?" her voice quivered.

Lance shook his head, lips curving into a smirk. "It's your fault for looking," he chuckled, casually taking the phone. "You have no business going through a man's phone. You hurt your own feelings."

Angela's heart clenched at his words. "You're supposed to be a man of God..."

"I AM A MAN OF GOD!!!" he roared, eyes filling with rage. "Don't forget your place! You are here to serve me! Nothing more!"

"You're a hypocrite!" she mumbled, the words barely audible.

"That's fine!" he spat. "I'll be a hypocrite! But God called me! Not you! So you don't get to tell me anything!" He stepped closer, towering over her as she kneeled on the cold tiles.

Unable to hold them back any longer, a waterfall of tears burst from her eyes, body shaking uncontrollably as she struggled to her feet. Her only thought was to escape this moment in time and get as far away from him as possible. She grabbed her purse and headed toward the front door. But before she could reach it, Lance grabbed her by the hair.

"LET ME GO!" She screamed, pain rippling through her scalp as she clawed at his hands to release her.

"AND WHERE THE HELL DO YOU THINK YOU'RE GO-ING???" he yelled, dragging her flailing body down the hall.

"LANCE STOP!" she cried. "WHAT ARE YOU DOING?"

He yanked her up and threw her across the bed. "You think you can just walk out on me?" he growled. "I own you!"

Angela watched in horror as he pulled rope from his bottom drawer. She attempted to run out of the door but he overpowered her.

"L...Lance! W..hat... are y..ooou d...d..doing?" she stuttered, struggling to get from beneath him.

After a few minutes of fighting to get control of her hands, he pinned her down, tying her wrists to the bedposts with swift, forceful movements, as if he had done this before. Panic surged through her as she thrashed against the restraints, her cries falling on deaf ears.

"Lance, let me go!" she begged. "Why are you doing this?"

"You will stay here," he paused, drawing in a deep steadying breath. "Until you are ready to be obedient!" He straightened his disheveled clothes and stormed out, slamming the door be-hind him.

"Lance? Lance??? LANCE!!!" she screamed frantically.

Minutes stretched into hours, her body stiffening with each passing second. The first night, she clung to hope, believing that surely he would come back, if not to untie her, then at least to check on her. But the hours continued to tick by, and the door remained closed. The creak of floorboards and the faint thud of footsteps in the distance made her heart leap with hope that he was finally coming. Be he never did.

By the second day, her body weakened as exhaustion set in. Hunger growled from her stomach and dehydration seized her throat. Her tears had long since dried, energy sapped by the endless hours of crying. Each time she tugged at the ropes, they tightened more, burning the raw skin around her wrists, bruising them from the constant struggle.

"Lance? I'm sorry," she rasped, hearing movement on the other side of the door. "Please let me go..." Only silence answered, followed by fading footsteps.

Hours later, she heard shuffling of pots and pans in the kitchen. She strained to listen, her senses heightened by the emptiness pulling at her stomach. The sound of sizzling butter followed by the unmistakable smell of garlic frying in the pan hit her nose. Then came the smell of onions, their pungency mellowed out by the heat. Her mind raced, trying to figure out what was being prepared. She imagined chicken, roasted to perfection as rosemary, thyme, and lemon pepper wafted through the house. It was the kind of dish Lance loved. The thought of the juicy, browned skin crisping in the oven made her mouth water despite the dryness in her throat. Angela's weakened heart fluttered in desperate hope as she imagined warm, soft rolls, freshly baked, their crusts golden and crisp, slathered with butter. The mingling smells of herbs and roasting meat was a cruel taunt to her starving body.

Maybe he's cooking for me... she hoped, glancing repeatedly at the door. "Lance?" she whispered, barely able to speak.

But the minutes dragged on, and no footsteps came to the door. The smell of the meal grew stronger, filling every corner of the room until it felt suffocating, a mockery of her suffering. She closed her eyes, trying to push the hunger away, but it was sharp and insistent. When the sun began to set, she heard a faint, distinct sound of a woman's laughter flowing from the dining room, mixed with the hum of conversation and the clinking of utensils.

"LANCE!" she squeaked, heart dropping at the realization someone else was there enjoying a meal with her husband while he had her tied up.

After a couple of hours, the distant clink of dishes being put away faded and the house fell silent. Angela lay still, her arms throbbing as the ropes bit further into her wrists. Suddenly, the silence was pierced by a new sound—muffled grunts and low moans. She gasped, struggling to process what she was hearing. Her husband's grunts grew louder, it was a sound she knew all too well. They were coming from the guest bedroom down the hall, intertwined with a woman's soft whimpers of pleasure. Angela's stomach turned in disbelief and fury.

"God... why are you allowing this to happen?" she prayed, staring at the ceiling, a single tear dropping from her dry eyes. Her mind went blank in shock, her body paralyzed in a nightmare she couldn't wake up from.

By day three, her body was limp, her mind floating between brief moments of fitful sleep and a dazed state of confusion. She had lost track of time and the pain in her wrist was now numb. Lance didn't visit once. No water... No food... No words... Her agonizing hunger was replaced by despair, an ever-growing void in the pit of her stomach. She wanted to scream, to beg for mercy, but she had no energy left. All she could do was lie there, staring at the ceiling, wondering how her life had come to this. Wondering if he would ever come back at all. Wondering if she would die here.

As the sun began to set, the door slowly creaked open, the sound barely registering. Footsteps echoed softly against the floorboards as Lance entered the room. He sat beside her on the bed, the mattress sinking slightly under his weight.

"Are you ready to be obedient?"

Angela managed to lift her head slightly, body too feeble to fight anymore. She gave a small, almost imperceptible nod, her spirit crushed beneath the weight of submission.

"Good!" he kissed her forehead. "I figured if God could end Jesus' suffering after three days, I could give you another chance."

He untied her hands and lifted her frail body into his arms with a gentleness that was eerily out of place given the days of torment she had just endured. Angela's head hung limply, her mind still foggy as he carried her into the adjoining bathroom. A fresh bouquet of pink roses awaited her and a warm water filled the tub, surrounded by lavender candles. Lance removed her clothing and lowered her into the water. She winced, feeling the rushing sensation of relief flood her aching limbs. He turned on some soft music and began to bathe her, gently rubbing the cloth over her malnourished skin. Grabbing the first aid kit, he bandaged her wrist, hiding away the evidence of her suffering.

"Mrs. Mary heard you weren't feeling well and brought by some groceries," he continued as he dried his hands. "Get yourself cleaned up and make me some dinner." Before leaving the bathroom, he paused at the door. "Next time you speak against me, I will kill you." He didn't wait for a response. He didn't need one. The door clicked shut behind him, leaving her alone in the romantically decorated bathroom.

Angela stared blankly at the wall, her mind too overwhelmed to process the cruelty she had just endured. She knew she had no choice but to obey. She would get up, clean herself, and make dinner as he commanded. As the bathwater cooled, she reached for the card that sat by the roses. It was small with gold trim along the edges and her name was written in Lance's bold handwriting across the front. She tore it open slowly, her mind already dreading whatever cruel message lay inside. Her heart pounded as she unfolded the card.

'Til death do us part!' was written inside.

A faint depleted gasp escaped her throat. Those words, once a vow, were now a threat. The meaning was clear, there was no escape. Sinking into the water, she closed her eyes, feeling empty, terrified, and trapped.

That was the first and last time she ever spoke against her husband.

Lance raised his arms, his voice growing louder, signaling the close of his sermon. Angela sighed as the choir began to sing their final hymn. Her shoulders slumped under the burden of the act she had to perform week after week. The loneliness inside her grew thicker, suffocating her, the hidden truth becoming unbearable to hold. She wondered how long she could keep pretending before she broke.

After the service, Angela moved through the crowd, smiling and exchanging pleasantries with the members, though her heart wasn't in it. The warmth of the congregation, the handshakes, and well-wishes only deepened the disconnection she felt. As she reached the back of the church, Denise, her best friend, caught up with her.

"Angela, hey girl," she gently touched her arm.

"Hey!" Angela exclaimed softly, reaching out to hug her friend.

"Now, I know you said you're alright but I'm going to keep asking. You've been acting so distant lately."

"I'm fine," she replied quickly, forcing a smile, the kind that came so easily now.

"You sure? Because I've been thinking—either you're stressed, or maybe... you're pregnant?" Denise let out a small laugh, trying to lighten the mood.

"Denise!" Angela shrieked, pulling her friend to the side. "Don't even joke like that! You know Lance doesn't want kids!" she whispered, eyes darting around for any sign of her husband or eavesdroppers.

"Oh, shoot, Angie! I forgot. I'm so sorry girl. I didn't mean to upset you. I just worry, you know?"

"I know, I know. Just don't ever let him hear you say that, please!"

Seeing her friend look and sound so fearful, Denise's face dropped to a concerned frown. "You know you can talk to me about anything, right?" she squeezed her hand. "I mean that, Ange. You have always been there for me, and I hope you know I'm here for you too."

Angela's throat tightened at her words. For a split second, she considered telling her everything. But she couldn't. Not here, not now.

"Thanks, Denise. I appreciate it," she nodded, forcing another smile.

Denise stared at her for a moment longer, trying to read her face. "Alright sweetie, well just remember, I am only a phone call away," she smiled, hugged her, and walked toward the exit. "I love you!" she yelled, without turning around.

Weaving through a sea of people, searching for her husband, a familiar face caught her eye. It was Tasha. The glowing woman stood near the side entrance, waving as some young ladies gravitated toward her. Angela's heart skipped a beat, stomach tightening in dread. Tasha hadn't been at the church for over a month, and Angela allowed herself to believe her affair with Lance had ended.

"Ooohs" and "ahhs" suddenly rang out, followed by laughter and excited cheers as the crowd that gathered around Tasha buzzed with congratulatory energy. Angela instinctively moved closer, trying to see what all the fuss was about.

And then she saw it.

Tasha's hands rested on a very swollen pregnant belly. *Pregnant?* Angela stopped dead in her tracks, heart dropping into her stomach, the realization hitting her like a punch to the gut. And if she had to guess, the timing lined up perfectly to be anyone else's child. She felt lightheaded as she stood frozen watching the scene unfold. Tasha's gaze flickered toward her. As their eyes met for a brief second, something unspoken passed between them. A smug smile played across Tasha's face as she rubbed her belly.

"Oh... Hi, First Lady!"

Angela's body went rigid, her voice catching in her throat. Her lips parted but no words came out. She glanced down at Tasha's belly again, she could barely breathe. "I–" she started, but the words felt strangled, caught in a web of disbelief and rage. Thinking quickly, she grabbed her phone, pretended to answer a call, and walked off. Tasha's smile didn't falter. In fact, it grew, almost as if she were daring Angela to say something.

"Do you need anything else, or can I go home?" Angela asked, walking into Lance's office, fighting back tears.

"Did something happen?" he paused, noticing the tears filling her eyes. His brow furrowed slightly, though not in concern—more in curiosity.

Angela was unsure of what to say. Rubbing her scarred wrists, her mind raced back to the days she spent tied to the bed. She knew better than to push him and decided to not test her boundaries.

"I... I, uh," she stammered, clearing her throat, searching for an answer. "I stubbed my toe on the pew."

"You are so clumsy." he chuckled, shaking his head. "You may go. Oh... don't worry about dinner. I will be eating out tonight. Don't wait up for me," he added, turning his attention back to the papers on his desk.

She could feel the tears threatening to spill over, her emotions barely held together by the thinnest thread of self-control. Eating out. She knew exactly what that meant and who he was likely planning to meet. The image of Tasha's pregnant belly flashed through her mind. She swallowed hard, forcing herself to keep the tears at bay.

"Okay," she whispered.

Angela's breath came in shallow and quick gasps as she made her way down the corridor, the sounds of the congregation still lingering faintly in the background. The cool breeze hit her face as she pushed through the exit door, but it did nothing to ease the suffocating pressure in her chest. She stood outside for a moment, clutching her purse tightly against her body.

You know you can talk to me about anything, right?

Denise's words echoed through her mind. Denise had always been her rock, her confidante, someone who provided both emotional and spiritual support when Angela needed it most.

For years they had shared everything, but now, as she stood alone, she struggled to reveal the darkest parts of her marriage. She didn't want to pretend any longer. The thought of confiding in her, of finally unburdening herself, made her both anxious and desperate. Could she trust Denise with this truth? Would she even believe her?

Angela took a deep breath, unlocked her car door, and slipped inside. She gripped the steering wheel, her knuckles turning white as she fought the urge to scream. After wrestling with the ideas, she finally picked up her phone and selected Denise's number. Each ring stretched endlessly, and with every passing second, Angela considered hanging up, retreating into silence. Just as she was about to lose her nerve, Denise answered.

"Angie! Hey girl."

"Heeeey... are you busy? Can we meet?"

"Of course, hun. You okay?"

"I...I just need to talk to you. It's important."

"Why don't you just come by my house on your way home from church? I cooked."

"Okay, thank you. I'm on my way now."

The short drive to Denise's house felt like miles, her mind racing with a thousand thoughts as she navigated through familiar streets. *What if she didn't understand? What if telling her just makes it worse?* Pulling into Denise's driveway, Angela turned off the car and sat there for a moment. She gripped the steering wheel one more time, steadying herself for what was to come. With a deep breath, she opened the car door and stepped out, heart pounding as she inched to the front door.

Before she could knock, the door swung open, and her friend stood there with a warm smile. "Come on in," she said softly, pulling her into a hug. "Let's talk."

As Angela stepped into the warmth of her, the comforting atmosphere did little to ease the tightness in her chest. The familiar scent of roasted potatoes, vegetables and spices filled the air, mingling with the soft hum of music playing in the background.

"Come sit down," Denise said, guiding her toward the kitchen table where two plates were already set. "I made enough for both of us." She pulled out a chair and gestured for Angela to sit.

Angela offered a weak smile as she took a seat, eyes flickering around the room, searching for some distraction, anything to stop the flood of emotions threatening to spill over. She felt exposed, vulnerable, like a dam about to break.

Denise sat across from her, her gaze gentle but probing, clearly sensing that something was deeply wrong. She reached across the table and took Angela's hand, giving it a reassuring squeeze. "Whatever it is, you know you can tell me. I'm here for you."

"I don't even know where to start," Angela whispered, her voice cracking slightly.

"Start wherever you feel comfortable."

Angela hesitated for a moment, then reached into her purse and pulled out her phone. Her hands trembled as she unlocked the screen and found the incriminating screenshots of the messages she had discovered on Lance's phone. She bit her lip, took a shaky deep breath, and handed her the phone.

Denise's eyes widened in disbelief as she flipped through the messages. Her face turned pale, then, her expression shifted to simmering rage.

"That mother—" her lips tightened, as she tried to hold back the flood of emotions. "Oh, this is a mess!" she sighed, setting the phone on the table. "I can't believe he would do this. To you, to the church!"

"I know," she whispered. "But what do I do, Denise?"

"I know this is hard, but you have an obligation to expose him. The congregation deserves to know the truth. You can't protect him at the expense of your own soul."

Angela swallowed hard, her mind racing with conflicting emotions. "I feel stuck... like if I speak up, I'm the one destroying everything."

"You need to be honest. It will be difficult, and people will be hurt, but in the end, it's the right thing to do."

Angela leaned back in her chair, the weight of her friend's words sinking in. Deep down, she knew Denise was right. As painful as it would be, she had an ethical and moral duty not just to herself but to the community she had served alongside Lance.

Denise squeezed Angela's hand tightly, "I'll stand by you, Angela. Whatever you decide."

"T.T., milk!" a tiny boy, no more than three years old shuffled into the kitchen, rubbing his eyes.

"Oh!" Angela jumped. "Who's this?"

Denise laughed, standing up to grab a cup from the counter. "This is Marcus, my cousin's son. I'm babysitting for the week."

Angela's eyes followed the toddler as he stumbled over to Denise, watching with curiosity as he climbed into her arms. There was something about him that looked oddly familiar. *He kinda looks like...* She stopped herself, shaking her head quickly. *No. No. That is ridiculous. You're overthinking.* She forced herself to push the thought aside.

"You okay?" Denise asked, noticing the faraway look in Angela's eyes as she returned to the table.

"Yeah... yeah, I'm fine," she replied, though the lingering thought still hovered in the back of her mind, no matter how hard she tried to dismiss it. "Let me get out of here so he can relax," she said grabbing her phone and headed toward the door.

"Okay, hun!" Denise followed her. "You know, no matter what happens, you've already taken the first step by telling someone."

Angela smiled but as she glanced back at the small boy nestled in her arms, a cold shiver ran down her spine. She shook it off again, telling herself she was just imagining things. It was impossible.

Wasn't it?

Over the next week, Angela moved through her days in a haze, her mind consumed by the decision she had made to expose Lance's infidelity to the church. Each morning she woke the knot of anxiety in her stomach grew, her thoughts racing the moment her eyes opened. At night, she sat alone in bed, rehearsing the words in her mind, playing through different scenarios, imagining how it would all unfold.

"I can't stay silent anymore. You deserve to know the truth," she whispered, practicing in front of the mirror.

There were times when her hands would shake uncontrollably as she imagined standing before the congregation. Would they turn on her, accusing her of destroying the church? Would they refuse to believe her, loyal to the man they had admired for so long? These thoughts plagued her, amplifying the anxiety churning inside her. To shatter their illusion meant losing everything she had known for the past ten years.

One afternoon, she went and stood in the empty church. She looked out over the row of pews and imagined the moment she would step forward to speak. The thought of it made her feel physically ill, but deep down, she knew this was her only way forward. She couldn't go back to pretending everything was perfect when her life had been crumbling.

Denise had been a lifeline, texting and calling her every day to offer reassurance and support. "You're doing the right thing, Angie," she'd say. "This isn't just about you—it's about the truth. And people deserve the truth, even if it hurts." Angela clung to those words, repeating them to herself whenever the fear threatened to overtake her.

As the week drew to a close, she found it harder to eat. *I will kill you...* Echoed repeatedly in her mind when she imagined Lance's reaction the moment he found out. He had no idea what was coming. He still moved around the house with his usual air of arrogance, treating her with the same indifference he always did, unaware that his life was about to change forever. The night before Sunday morning service, Angela sat in her room, staring at the small notebook where she had written out her speech. Her hands trembled as she tapped the words with her finger, reading them over and over again. She had written and rewritten her message countless times, trying to find the balance between honesty and dignity, between exposing the truth and not letting her own emotions overwhelm her.

The next morning as she made her way to the church, she knew that after today, her world would be irrevocably changed. She could feel the tension mounting as she walked through the doors, her pulse quickening with each step. As morning scriptures, prayers, and hymns came and went, Angela tapped her foot waiting for the right moment to deliver her message.

Just as she stood and turned to face the people, she froze seeing Tasha walk in, proudly showing her swollen belly and cradling the same little boy she saw at Denise's house. Her heart stopped, and for a brief dizzying moment, she felt the room tilt. Angela locked eyes with Tasha, who quickly averted her gaze.

"Excus–"

"May I have your attention, please?" Denise suddenly rose from her seat, cutting Angela off. "I have some heartbreaking news to share."

Confusion rippled through the crowd as people began to whisper, shifting uncomfortably in their seats. Lance furrowed his brows as he stood at the podium, preparing to bring forth his sermon. His eyes darted from Denise to Angela as he tried to piece together what was happening.

What was Denise doing? She thought, clutching the edge of her seat, as panic surged through her.

"Our Reverend Lance Brown has been involved in sinful acts that betray not just his family, but also, our community!"

"LIES!" Lance yelled, throwing a fist in the air. "Be gone from here devil!"

Echoes of gasps spread through the pews as people turned to one another in confusion, disbelief, and horror.

"And I have proof!" Denise continued, pointing at the large screen behind the pulpit.

One by one, photos of Lance and Tasha appeared. In some, they were holding hands, and others were still shots of intimate moments. The final image was of Tasha holding her engorged belly, Lance standing behind her, his hand resting possessively on her stomach, and little Marcus beside them.

"This relationship has been going on for years," she said, her tone cold and unwavering. "And for those wondering how I received this information... Tasha is my cousin!"

A deafening silence fell over the room as all eyes fell on Lance, whose face was drained of color. His eyes narrowed in fury at Angela, but she could only stare back, equally stunned. His mouth opened, but no words came. The disbelief clouding his features quickly morphed into anger, his face twisting with rage as he glanced back at Denise. Tasha sank in her pew, wishing to be anywhere but here. She wrapped her arms protectively around her son, trying to shield him from the judgment pouring in from every direction. Angela couldn't move, couldn't speak. The devastation cut too deep. She had confided in Denise and she had known all along. The air turned icy, thick with betrayal and disbelief. People began murmuring loudly, the shock turning to outbursts of anger and confusion. Everything was unraveling.

After most of the sanctuary had cleared out, Angela spotted Denise speaking animatedly with a group of church members and pulled her to the side.

"You stole my moment, Denise, why?"

Denise glanced around to ensure no one was listening. "I wanted to be the one to expose Lance," she whispered. "To claim the moral high ground. I've been talking to the church board for the last few years and they fully support me taking over as the next spiritual leader here! Isn't that exciting?" she squealed, her eyes gleaming with a twisted sense of victory.

Angela's mouth fell open. "I..I... I don't understand," her voice trembled, rage building inside her. "So, you used my misery for your ambition? And... And Tasha? Your cousin? You knew what he was doing all this time?!?!"

"Oh, please, Angela. Don't act so shocked. I knew Lance was a dog years ago. He was always charming, but I saw the way he looked at other women. So I told my cousin to get close to him, to seduce him. It was all part of the plan. I needed proof of his sins to take him down. Tasha was supposed to help me get the evidence I needed to force him out, but she ruined everything by falling in love with him. Then she had the nerve to refuse to give me what I needed!" Denise's eyes flashed with frustration, her smile dropping momentarily. "I never anticipated her getting pregnant."

"I can't believe you!"

"You really should be thanking me, ya know…"

"Thank–," Angela recoiled, shocked, at her audacity. "I thought you were my friend."

"Friendship is subjective, Angela." she shrugged. "And this isn't all that bad. We got rid of the trash, didn't we? Lance is out, and now you can help me right this ship."

"You're crazy," Angela shook her head, feeling sick.

"Crazy? No, Angela. Ambitious. A visionary, even. And if you had any sense, you'd see the opportunity here. And you know what they say…. sometimes, blessings come from the most un-expected places."

THE END

Karma's Kitchen

Karma's Kitchen was buzzing with life, an upscale hotspot that blended Southern soul food with a Caribbean twist. Warm amber lights bathed the polished tables, and the low hum of conversation filled the air, punctuated by the occasional burst of laughter. The walls were adorned with eclectic art and historical jazz musicians that captured the essence of the South and the islands. The sweet smoky aroma of jerk chicken, collard greens, and fried plantains lingered in the air, tempting every guest who walked through the door.

This wasn't just a restaurant, it was an experience. From the moment guests arrived, they were met with impeccable service, exotic cocktails, and food prepared with love. The clinking of glasses, the rhythm of music playing softly overhead, and the sight of celebrities enjoying their meals all contributed to the lively atmosphere. Reservations had to be made weeks in advance and on any given night, you might find a famous actress in one corner, a Grammy-winning musician in another, and a sports star taking pictures with fans by the bar. Karma's Kitchen was the place to be seen, a social media darling, its dishes frequently snapped and shared by influencers and foodies alike.

With her dazzling smile and magnetic charm, Jayla worked the room like a natural. Dressed to the nines, she greeted guests by name, made sure the VIP tables were attended to, and always found time to stop for a quick chat or selfie with a celebrity. She was the perfect hostess, effortlessly mingling and ensuring that everyone had the time of their lives.

While the dining room was a stage of elegance and sophistication, the kitchen was a battlefield. Jay stood at the helm, directing his team with the precision of a general. The air was thick with heat, the scent of sautéing garlic and the sharp sizzle of frying pans filled the room. Orders flew in faster than they could be sent out, and the staff moved in a perfectly choreographed dance to get plates ready and served. Steam hissed from pots, knives chopped rhythmically, and the calls for orders echoed through the space. This was Jay's domain but behind the glitz and glamour, in the sweltering heat of the kitchen, he felt invisible.

The restaurant was his vision, his dream, but no one seemed to remember that. When the food was praised, it was Jayla who was thanked. When celebrities tweeted about their fantastic meals, it was Jayla who got tagged. She was always the one interviewed, her face on the covers of local magazines, talking about their "shared" success. He had poured his heart and soul into every detail, the ingredients, the recipes, and the flavors that blended perfectly to create something extraordinary. But in the eyes of the public, he was just the guy in the kitchen, out of sight and out of mind. Jay knew she worked hard, but there was a sting in seeing his contributions reduced to nothing more than a footnote in the restaurant's accomplishments.

As Jay stirred the pot of his signature gumbo, he glanced through the pass window to where Jayla was entertaining a table of high-profile guests. She looked radiant in her form-fitting, deep red dress as her laughter rang out like music, loud and vibrant, as she effortlessly charmed everyone around her. Jay's grip tightened on the ladle as it moved through the thick stew, blending the tender chunks of shrimp, sausage, and okra. The sight of her soaking up all the attention twisted something inside of him. His chest tightened in anger as he watched her. For years he told himself it was fine, he didn't care about being in the spotlight, he enjoyed working in the background. But deep down he wanted more acknowledgment.

"Hey, Chef, you good?" asked a familiar voice, snapping him out of his thoughts, as the door to the kitchen creaked open.

Jay spun around, his expression shifting as he saw Serena leaning casually against the doorframe, arms crossed with a playful smirk on her lips. Her red hair was pinned up elegantly, and she wore a fitted black dress that hugged her curves in all the right places.

"Serena!" he said softly. "What are you doing back here? You know Jayla doesn't like–"

She waved a dismissive hand before he could finish. "Forget about Jayla," she interrupted, closing the door behind her. "I just had your gumbo. It's even better than I remembered." She licked her lips.

As she approached him slowly, Jay bit his lip, smelling her intoxicating perfume. Every time she came around, he couldn't help but be drawn in by her presence.

"You really are a genius, you know that?" she said rubbing her fingers over his chest. "Every bite was perfection. The best gumbo I've ever had."

"T...Thanks, Serena," he said trying to keep his tone casual.

"You know you're the real star of this place."

"It doesn't feel that way," he mumbled, glancing at Jayla, raising her glass for another toast.

"Then maybe it's time for you to step out of the shadows," she whispered. "Time for you to build something that's all yours, where you get the credit you deserve."

His pulse quickened at her words. "And where exactly does that leave you?"

Serena smiled, eyes gleaming. "Right there beside you," she replied. "Partners. Equals. I wouldn't let you do it alone."

Her words hung in the air, thick with possibility. Jay knew he was playing with fire, but part of him didn't care. For too long, he had been nothing more than the man behind the scenes, his hard work eclipsed by Jayla's growing empire. Maybe Serena was right. Maybe it was time for him to claim what was his.

"You don't have to keep being invisible, Jay," she said softly, sauntering toward the door. "You deserve more than that."

Their affair began shortly after that night. It started with late-night conversations, stolen moments in the back alley where they could talk without being overheard, and secret texts that Jay found himself waiting for eagerly. Serena made him feel seen and lifted him in ways Jayla hadn't done in years. The first kiss was inevitable. It happened after a long night at the restaurant while she helped him close. They told themselves it wouldn't go any further, that it was just a one-time thing. But like the gumbo Jay made, once the ingredients were mixed, there was no undoing it. They found themselves seeking each other out and looking for excuses to be alone, the thrill of secrecy giving them a rush neither of them could resist.

It wasn't just the physical connection that kept Jay coming back to Serena. It was the way she made him feel important. She wasn't just praising his cooking, she praised him. She saw his ambition, heard his frustrations, and acknowledged his need to be more than Jayla's shadow. Serena fueled those desires and whispered in his ear about the life and success he could have if he just reached out and took it.

And Jay did imagine it. He pictured himself as the face of a new restaurant—his restaurant. Where people would come for his food, his vision. He would be the one interviewed by the press and showcased on magazine covers. It was a fantasy that consumed him more and more with each passing day.

Soon, Serena said it was time to open their own restaurant, a place that would rival Karma's Kitchen. She had the connections, investors looking to back a fresh concept, and suppliers willing to switch allegiances for the right deal. It would be a bold move, but Serena made it sound so easy. And the more Jay thought about it, the more tempting it became. He found himself pulling away from Jayla, both emotionally and physically. Their once-strong partnership was now strained, conversations limited to business transactions and logistics. Jayla didn't notice at first, too caught up in expanding the brand and securing deals. She was always on the phone, always in meetings, and always hustling for the next big thing. All while Jay was slipping further and further into Serena's orbit. One night, after Jay and Serena had gone over potential locations for the new restaurant, he returned home to find Jayla sitting in the living room, eyes glued to her laptop. She glanced up as he walked in.

"You're home late," she yawned. "Busy night at the restaurant?"

"Yeah," he replied nervously, pulling off his jacket. "You know how it is... always something to fix."

She didn't respond, her focus was already back on the computer. Jay hovered in the doorway and watched her work. This was the woman he had built his life with, the woman he had once been madly in love with. He felt guilty but all he could see now was the growing distance between them.

"Jayla," he mumbled, rubbing his head as he hovered in the doorway.

"Hmm?" she responded, eyes never leaving the screen.

"Uh... never mind," he sighed and walked away.

While Serena continued to plot Jay's escape, Jayla was too focused on the business to notice the cracks forming beneath her. But she wasn't completely oblivious. At first, when Jay started coming home late more often, she barely blinked. She assumed he was spending extra time at the restaurant, making sure everything was perfect. After all, that's what he always did. He was the kind of chef who didn't leave until the kitchen was spotless, the staff was ready for the next day, and the last dish had been scrubbed clean. She didn't question the occasional secretive phone call or the way he seemed irritated when they talked. If anything, she chalked it up to the stress of running the business. Karma's Kitchen was a beast that never slept, and the demands on them were never-ending.

But over time, Jayla started to notice little things that didn't quite add up. Jay's once-consistent routine began to shift. He was taking longer breaks, disappearing for hours, and his phone was always in his hand. He was more distant and less engaged when they discussed plans for the restaurant's future. His once affectionate demeanor had become cold, his conversations clipped. She found herself lying awake at night, staring at his empty side of the bed, wondering what had changed between them. Jayla wanted to believe that it was just the strain of the business, that maybe they had grown too comfortable in their roles, and the passion they once shared was buried beneath the weight of their success. But the more she thought about it, her gut told her something was wrong. Jay wasn't just tired...he was hiding something.

The following Tuesday night, Jayla stayed late at the restaurant for a meeting. She hadn't told Jay, hoping to surprise him by finalizing a lucrative deal that would expand Karma's Kitchen globally. As she locked up and walked toward the kitchen, she heard talking coming from the back office. It was a woman's voice, followed by Jay's. Jayla stopped in her tracks, heart pounding as she edged closer, careful not to make a sound. The door was slightly ajar enough that she could hear them clearly.

"You just need to get through the next couple of weeks," Serena said. "Once we've secured the location, you'll be out of here before she realizes what's happening!"

"Wow! A place that's all mine... I mean ours. All ours!" Jay said with an excitement Jayla hadn't heard in months.

Jayla's blood ran cold. It took everything in her not to storm in there and confront them. She wanted to scream, to tear into Jay for betraying her, for lying to her face. But she wasn't the kind of woman who let her emotions control her. She had built her career on being calm, strategic, and always one step ahead of the game. So, she did what she did best...strategize.

About two weeks later, Jay found Jayla at her desk in their shared office. She didn't even look up when he entered the room, her face bathed in the usual glow of her laptop. He felt a pang of guilt but he pushed it down, reminding himself that this was about his future. Clearing his throat, he inched closer.

"Jayla... we need to talk."

"What's up?" she looked up, arching an eyebrow.

"I...I, uh, I'm opening my own restaurant."

For a brief second, her face remained impassive. She leaned back in her chair, folding her arms across her chest. "Your own restaurant?" she repeated. "So, you're leaving Karma's Kitchen?"

"Not exactly," Jay said quickly, trying to soften the blow. "But Serena and I—"

"Serena!?!?" Jayla snapped, narrowing her eyes. "I told you that woman was a snake, Jay."

"She really isn't that bad... and... I just wanted to be honest with you about it."

Jayla rolled her eyes and stared at him, her expression unreadable. She didn't say anything for what felt like an eternity and Jay's nerves began to unravel. Finally, she stood up and approached him.

"Well... I can't stop you. I just hope you know what you're doing." She extended her hand. "Congratulations on your new business venture."

"Uh... r...really?" He exhaled, releasing a breath he didn't realize he was holding. "Thank you for being so understanding!" He shook her hand vigorously. "Will you come to the grand opening? It's next Friday."

"Of course, not!" she laughed, throwing her head back at his audacity. "But I'll see you at home, later. I have to hire a chef."

The week passed in a blur as Serena and Jay finalized the last-minute details. He poured everything into this venture, draining his savings, and taking out loans, betting it all on Serena's projected return on investments. The stakes were high, but he believed it was worth it. She assured him that the investors were excited, the staff was prepped, and the suppliers were ready. Everything was in place.

On the night of the grand opening, Jay stood in front of the double doors of his new restaurant, heart pounding with pride as he looked at the name 'Jay's Place' in neon letters. Serena was beside him, beaming with confidence as they welcomed the first few guests inside. Jay had spent all day preparing his signature gumbo, the dish that had helped build his reputation. It was going to be the centerpiece of the evening. But as hours passed, the initial excitement began to sour. The restaurant was far from full and the handful of guests looked uncomfortable waiting to be served. The staff Serena had guaranteed had never showed up. Jay rushed to the kitchen to plate up bowls of gumbo for his supporters.

"Thanks for coming! I appreciate your support." He greeted, passing out orders.

He looked at Serena pacing near the front, phone glued to her ear. Her calm demeanor had vanished replaced by a desperation she couldn't hide.

"What do you mean you can't make it?" she hissed, glancing at Jay, eyes wide in panic. "NO! We had a deal!" She ended the call abruptly, frantically dialing another, fingers shaking as she pushed the keys. "What happened to the staff? They were confirmed for tonight!" she snapped. "Where the hell are they?"

"We can't serve half the menu without the fresh ingredients!" Jay whispered to her, starting to regret his decision.

"I'm trying to get a hold of them! I don't know what's going on, but no one is answering! It's like everyone just vanished! I swear I had everything lined up!"

And just when he thought things couldn't get any worse... Jayla walked in.

"Wha...What are you doing here?" Jay stuttered.

"You really thought I would miss your big night, honey?" she smiled smugly, her gaze drifting around the half-empty restaurant and landing on the bowls of gumbo. "You know you can't serve that right?"

"What do you mean?" he blinked in confusion.

Jayla reached into her sleek black purse and pulled out a folded document. She held it between her fingers like a well-played card in a game she had already won. Jay's blood ran cold when he saw it. He recognized it immediately.

"The contract you signed when we started Karma's Kitchen. Remember?" she asked, carefully unfolding the pages, scanning them as she spoke. "Here! It states any signature dishes created during our partnership at Karma's Kitchen, including, but not limited to, that gumbo, belong exclusively to the restaurant. You signed over your rights, Jay. And according to this, you can't cook or sell that recipe anywhere else without my permission."

His face went pale and his chest tightened. "I–"

"WHAT?" Serena shrieked. "Yo...you didn't tell me about this!" she screamed, punching him in the arm. "This can't be real!"

"Oh, it's real honey, but don't worry. I called all of your investors, suppliers, and potential partners and informed them of our standing contract. You know, to make sure Jay wouldn't get himself into more legal trouble than he anticipated. Because, let's be honest, that would all fall back on me." She let out a small humorless laugh. "Uh, and you're welcome!"

Jay's stomach dropped, he had been so focused on escaping Jayla's shadow that he had been careless and blindsided by his ambition. Jayla stepped back, her smile as sharp as ever, watching with satisfaction as the two of them floundered in the wreckage of their failed plans.

"Well, I'm sure you two have a lot to discuss!" she smirked, turned on her heels, and walked toward the door. "Oh, and Jay," she paused, casting one last look over her shoulder. "I want a divorce."

He stood there speechless, his mind spinning in a thousand different directions, heart heavy with the weight of his downfall.

"Uh, excuse me, sir," an older man tapped him on the shoulder. "Sorry, to bother you but my gumbo is cold."

THE END

www.ingramcontent.com/pod-product-compliance
Lightning Source LLC
Chambersburg PA
CBHW052205150726
48002CB00003B/1125